ISLAND HERITAGE™
PUBLISHING
A DIVISION OF THE MADDEN CORPORATION

94-411 Kō'aki Street, Waipahu, Hawai'i 96797-2806
Orders: (800) 468-2800 • Information: (808) 564-8800
Fax: (808) 564-8877
islandheritage.com

ISBN 1-59700-244-5
First Edition, First Printing - 2007

DADDY LOVE? *what is*

WRITTEN BY JANE SHAPIRO • ILLUSTRATED BY DON ROBINSON

To the children of Hawai‘i
Jane Shapiro

ISLAND HERITAGE™
PUBLISHING

Daddy, what is love?

Love is in my smile since you became part of our *'ohana*.

2

3

Do you love me?

Very much.

How much?

I love you more than all the canoes riding the waves, all the lava bubbling in Kīlauea and all the hula dancers chanting to the sinking sunlight.

How long will you love me?

I will love you as long as the humpback whales slap their tails, the red-footed boobies dive for fish, and the *honu* paddle to shore.

What if I walked Poki, but Poki pulled hard
and ran away?

We'd search for Poki.

What if we couldn't find him?

I'd cry. But still, I would love you.

11

What if I ran and jumped at the beach? By accident, I kicked over our water and spilled it onto the sand?

Then we'd both be thirsty.

What if I ran and jumped at the beach and kicked sand in our lunch?

Then we'd be hungry, but I would love you.

What if high waves splashed, but I swam out anyway?

I'd shout, "Hey, Liko, back to shore!"

14

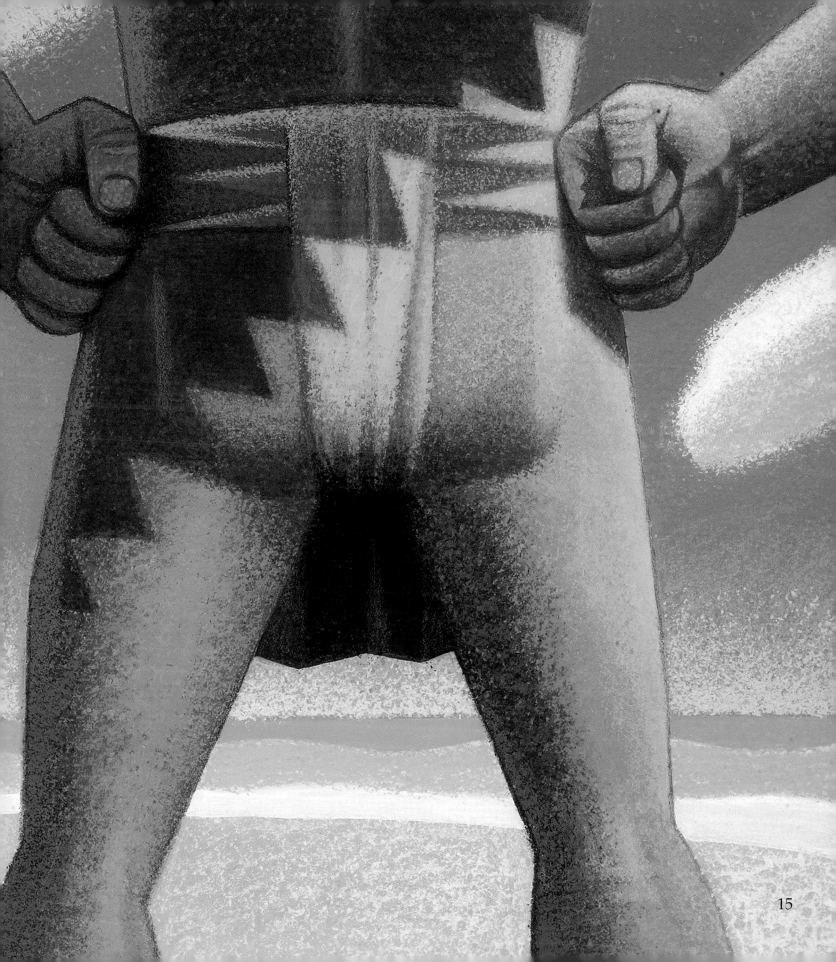

What if I kept swimming past the cliff?

Then I'd bring you back on my surfboard, and you wouldn't go in the ocean for a month.

I would not like what you did, but I would still love you.

What if I paddled in a race and dropped my paddle?

I'd watch you snatch it from the water.

What if I dropped my paddle and came in last?

First or last, I would love you, Liko.

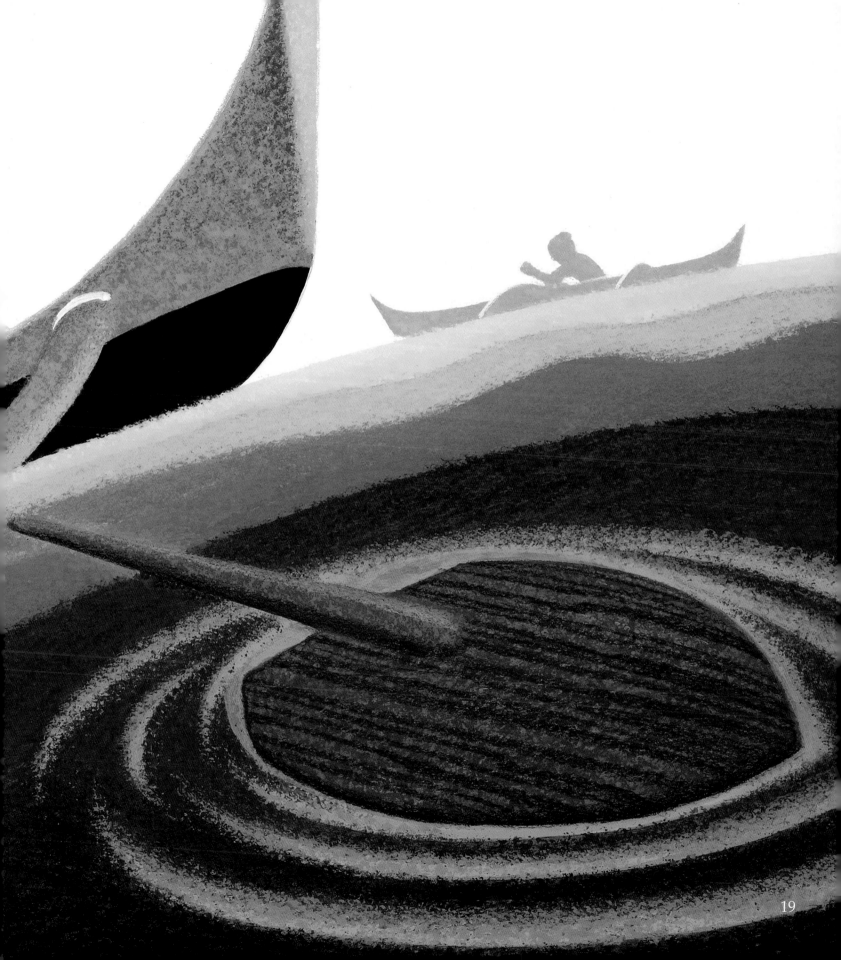

What if one day a tsunami crashed toward us
and I was scared?

I'd hold your hand and we'd run to the mountains.
You would feel me shaking, too.

20

What if a wild mountain pig charged me and flashed its teeth?

We'd climb an *'ōhi'a ai* tree and listen to the honeycreepers sing.

What if I fell from the tree and the pig twirled its tail,
whirled its snout at me, and drooled?

I'd scramble down and shake a stick at the pig's snout.

What if the pig still snarled?

I would wrestle the pig away from you, and then
we'd dig an *imu* to roast it.

We'd also pick mountain apples, and invite our *'ohana* to a *lū'au*.
And at our feast I would beam with love for you,
because I am your daddy and you are my Liko.

The End

GLOSSARY

Canoes–Polynesians settled the Hawaiian islands two thousand years ago, sailing across the ocean in outrigger canoes. Today many clubs paddle outrigger canoes in races.

Honeycreepers–For millions of years many species of honeycreepers searched for nectar (honey) in flowers. Now some of these endemic birds are extinct and some endangered. The *'ākohekohe* continue to creep on *'ōhi'a* trees in forests high atop Haleakalā on Maui.

Honu–This is the Hawaiian name for green sea turtles that may paddle close to shore. Keep your distance, though, honu are protected animals.

Hula dancers–*Hula kahiko* is the dance developed in Hawai'i by ancient Polynesians, probably for religious ceremonies, to honor the land, and to tell stories. Chants accompany movements and gestures. Today modern hula, *hula 'auana*, often is performed with music.

Humpback whales-(*na koholā*) These endangered whales arrive each winter to breed and to give birth in the warm ocean water around the Hawaiian islands. Before deep dives, they arch (hump) their backs.

Imu–These underground ovens lined with lava rocks are used for roasting whole pigs to serve at *lū'au*.

Kīlauea–This continually-erupting volcano slowly increases the size of Hawai'i Island as lava flows into the sea.

Liko–This Hawaiian name means a sparkling, newly opened leaf.

Lū'au–A feast of roasted pig and fruits of the islands, along with fish and vegetables, is served to *'ohana* and friends on special occasions.

'Ohana–The Hawaiian word for family. Family is important in Hawaiian culture. Families honor ancestors, respect grandparents, and include everyone.

'Ōhi'a–These trees grow fluffy red flowers that look like pompons. Early Hawaiians carved *'ōhi'a* wood into canoes.

'Ōhi'a 'ai–These mountain apples grow on trees in native forests. If you climb up a hill and into a forest, you may find mountain apples to pick.

Pigs–*Pua'a* were brought to Hawai'i by the earliest settlers. Wild pigs gobble native plants and leave mud puddles that breed mosquitoes.

Poki–A Hawaiian word for "boss," Poki is the name King Kamehameha I chose for his dog.

Red-footed boobies–(*'a*) Boobies are tropical seabirds that dive from high in the Hawaiian skies to snatch fish out of the water. Adult birds are white with red legs and feet and blue bills.

Tsunami-This wall of water may slam to shore after an earthquake on the ocean floor. The last tsunami to hit Hawai'i was in Hilo in 1960.